Mrs. Rosey Posey and the Baby Bird

story by Robin Jones Gunn

pictures by Christina Schofield

Right in the middle of Poppyville
at the end of Merry Lane
is a big yellow house.
Mrs. Rosey Posey lives here.
Children love Mrs. Rosey Posey.

One sunny day, Rachel heard
a small peep, peep, peep.

Rachel climbed up the apple tree
to see the baby bird.

The nest she found was empty.
"Where is the baby bird?" she asked.

Peep, peep, peep!

She saw the bird in the grass.

Rachel ran to get Mrs. Rosey Posey.

"A baby bird fell

out of the apple tree," said Rachel.

"Let's take it inside
and make a new nest,"
said Mrs. Rosey Posey.

Mrs. Rosey Posey fed the baby bird.

"I'm glad I found the bird.

No one else saw it," said Rachel.

"There is someone else who saw it,"

said Mrs. Rosey Posey.

Her eyes had a twinkle.

Her smile had a zing.

Mrs. Rosey Posey had a secret.

“Was it you?” asked Rachel.

“Did you see the bird fall?”

“No,” said Mrs. Rosey Posey.

“It is someone who lives here.
This someone cares
about every living thing.”
Rachel didn’t know who it was.

RP

The next day,
Ashley came with Rachel.
She wanted to see the bird.

“It’s so cute. May I feed it?”

asked Ashley.

Mrs. Rosey Posey gave her a bowl

full of squirmy worms.

Ashley made a face.

“I changed my mind,” she said.

After Mrs. Rosey Posey fed the bird, she took the girls out to the porch for a snack.

Mrs. Rosey Posey had a big bowl of candy worms waiting for them.

Rachel and Ashley laughed.
Then they peeped and cheeped
and ate the candy worms.

Rachel said, “Tell us the secret.
Who else knows about the baby bird?”
Mrs. Rosey Posey gave another clue.
“It’s someone who
knows all about you.”

“Is it my mom?” asked Ashley.

“No,” said Mrs. Rosey Posey.

The girls didn’t know who it was.

The next day, Bill came with Rachel.

He saw the baby bird in a bowl.

Mrs. Rosey Posey said,

"The baby bird likes this bath."

The bird shook its feathers.

The water sprayed Rachel and Bill.

Rachel said, “Please tell us.
Who knew that the bird fell?”
Mrs. Rosey Posey smiled.
“It’s someone who knows
what you are going to say
before you say it.”

“I know who it is,” said Bill.
“My grandma always knows when
I want a cookie before I ask her.”
“No,” said Mrs. Rosey Posey.
“It is not your grandma.
I’ll tell you the answer tomorrow.”

The next day,

Rachel came with Ashley and Bill.

Mrs. Rosey Posey smiled.

She was ready for a special day.
She picked up the baby bird
and led them to the top bedroom.

They went to the window.

"See if you can guess now

who else is watching this bird."

Mrs. Rosey Posey held up the bird.

“I know,” said Rachel. “It’s God!”

“Indeed,” said Mrs. Rosey Posey.

"Does he really know everything?"

asked Bill.

"Yes, he really does,"

said Mrs. Rosey Posey.

"God cares for us all."

Mrs. Rosey Posey

opened up her hands by the window.

The children watched.

The baby bird flew away.

All of them said, “Hooray!”